T0130332

# Lucy-Linn & the Laundromat Kittens

SANDRA HICKMAN SCHWABE

ILLUSTRATED BY ALI MITCHELL

AuthorHouse™
1663 Liberty Drive
Bloomington, IN 47403
www.authorhouse.com
Phone: 833-262-8899

Because of the dynamic nature of the Internet, any web addresses or links contained in this book may have changed since publication and may no longer be valid. The views expressed in this work are solely those of the author and do not necessarily reflect the views of the publisher, and the publisher hereby disclaims any responsibility for them.

This book is printed on acid-free paper.

Interior Image Credit: James Schwabe

ISBN: 978-1-6655-1173-5 (sc)
ISBN: 978-1-6655-1412-5 (hc)
ISBN: 978-1-6655-1172-8 (e)

Library of Congress Control Number: 2020925672

Print information available on the last page.

Published by AuthorHouse  01/15/2021

**author**HOUSE®

# Lucy-Linn & the Laundromat Kittens

**SANDRA HICKMAN SCHWABE**

ILLUSTRATED BY ALI MITCHELL

This little story was meant to be because of Ali, Jessie and Maverick.

Love and happiness,
From your Sandy

**Lucy-Linn** ran ahead of her mother as soon as they crossed the street. She always was first, because her mother always had a heavy cart full of clothes to be washed at the laundromat. As Lucy-Linn ran, she kept saying to herself, "I hope they are there; I hope they are there!"

Turning the corner, she suddenly stopped and looked at the big laundromat window. There, looking out at her, all in a row, were three kittens with their wet noses pressed up against the clean window.

Lucy-Linn laughed and clapped her hands. She walked along and slowly touched the glass where each little nose was pressed against the window. Emma, the first kitten, wrinkled up her little pink nose. Her long whiskers shook. Of all the kittens, she had the longest whiskers and the shortest tail. She was black as midnight, but her yellow eyes were always bright. To Lucy-Linn, she was a beautiful sight!

Next came a furry ball with brown tiger stripes. When Lucy-Linn pecked on the glass in front of the kitten's nose, she turned her head, opening one little blue eye. She slowly stood up, stretched her legs, and yawned a huge, huge yawn - the biggest yawn that Lucy-Linn had ever seen a kitten yawn!

Lucy-Linn said to the kitten, "Oh Grace, turn around so I can see your beautiful tail." Grace's tail was the softest and fluffiest, and Grace was very proud of it. After turning around to show all of her wondrous tail, she laid down, covered up her head, and fell back to sleep.

The last little nose belonged to the cutest kitten of all, whose name was Molly. She had white socks on her feet and green sparkling eyes. White spots dotted the rest of her fur, which was the softest of yellows. She loved to be sung to, and Lucy-Linn often did sing while waiting with her mother for the laundry to finish.

The kittens could hardly wait for Lucy-Linn to come inside to visit with them. They remembered her last visit. When she had smiled, she was missing one of her front teeth. She had told them that children lose their teeth when they turn a certain age and soon get brand new teeth. After Lucy-Linn had gone home that day, they crowded around their mother, Bertha, and they asked a thousand questions about children's teeth and kittens' teeth.

Today was going to be a special day. Lucy-Linn had told them that on her next visit she would pull out another loose tooth so they could see for themselves. As soon as she stepped inside, they all crowded around her and said, "is it today that your tooth will be coming out?"

Lucy-Linn looked at her mother and said, "I think so. Mother, are you almost finished with my tooth fairy pillow?"

Lucy-Linn's mother had been working on a wonderful pillow that Lucy-Linn could put her teeth on so the tooth fairy could leave a special present in return.

On hearing this, the kittens looked at each other and said, "A tooth fairy pillow? What is that? Please show us!"

The kittens ran over to where Lucy-Linn's mother was sitting to look at what she had in her hands. It was a small pillow and on top of it was a painted picture of Lucy-Linn smiling a big, gap-toothed smile. But where were her two front teeth? The kittens looked at Lucy-Linn standing beside them. She had only one front tooth missing, but her picture on the special pillow had two missing.

Lucy-Linn laughed because she knew just what the kittens were thinking. She and the kittens had always understood each other, even without words. As Lucy-Linn laughed, she felt something funny about her front tooth and got a serious look on her face. The kittens hadn't seen such a serious look before.

Lucy-Linn's mother approached her and gently put her hand up to Lucy-Linn's mouth as she looked inside. Lucy-Linn said, "Mother, I have been pushing back and forth on my loose tooth and it's ready to come out."

"Okay," said Mother, "let's try it."

With those words, her mother took a hold of the loose tooth and pulled. The tooth was slippery and it flew out from between her fingers!

Seeing the flying tooth, the kittens jumped to try to catch it; but a slippery, flying tooth, as we know, is very, very hard to catch.

It flew past Emma's long, long whiskers, making her sneeze; and when she sneezed, she blew the tooth into a large basket filled to the brim with Mrs. Vanny's clean clothes that had just come out of the dryer. Emma's bright eyes had followed the flying tooth, so she pointed her short tail toward the basket, telling her sisters just where to look.

Grace and Molly jumped into the basket filled to the brim with wonderful, sweet smelling, warm just-out-of-the-dryer clothes. Grace promptly sat down and wiggled deep into the warm clothes almost forgetting why she was there, but Molly didn't.

Using those four white, sock-clad feet, she dug here and there looking for Lucy-Linn's lost tooth. Meanwhile, sleepy Grace had snuggled deeper into the warm nest of clothes and suddenly felt something catch onto her fluffy tail. Flicking her tail, the tooth suddenly flew up and up into the air...

right into the open hands of a giggling Lucy-Linn!

Mrs. Vanny and Lucy-Linn's mother laughed and laughed until their sides hurt. "What funny and wonderful kittens they are," said Lucy-Linn's mother. "Mrs. Vanny, you are so lucky to have them and their mother, too."

Suddenly a sad look came upon Mrs. Vanny's face. "Whatever is the matter?" asked Lucy-Linn's mother.

"Well, the kittens are growing up and the cars travel up and down the street so fast that I am afraid something might happen to them. So, I will have to find them a new home very soon."

Hearing this, Lucy-Linn ran up to her mother. "Mother, mother, can we take them with us when we move into our new house in the country?"

"We will see," said Mother. "Let's talk it over with your father. Mrs. Vanny, can we tell you next week if we can take the kittens or not?"

"Yes, yes you can," Mrs. Vanny said. "I will keep my fingers crossed for you, Lucy-Linn."

Lucy-Linn already had her fingers and even her eyes crossed in the hope that her parents would say YES!

The next week came and all of the kittens were lined up at the laundromat's front window, waiting. They waited and waited all day until they had given up hope of ever seeing Lucy-Linn and her mother.

Emma saw it first. She saw the big moving truck coming around the corner with Lucy-Linn looking out of the window and waving her arms. Lucy-Linn jumped out of the truck as soon as her father had stopped; running up to the window as she smiled at each one of the three little kittens and their mother.

She ran in and gathered up all three kittens...

and looked at Bertha, the mommy cat, and said, "Mother and father said YES, YES, YES the kittens can come with us to live in our new house!"

Mrs. Vanny was happy and so was mommy cat Bertha, Emma, Grace, Molly, and most of all, Lucy-Linn.

Carrying the sweet little kittens in her arms to the seat of the truck, she placed them on a soft pillow that had been painted by Lucy-Linn and her mother. On the top of the pillow was a picture of three kittens surrounding a little girl and they were all smiling a smile with each one missing their two front teeth!

Lucy-Linn, Emma, Grace and Molly laughed and laughed at the funny picture of themselves. They knew that they would have many happy and fun adventures together.

## ABOUT THE AUTHOR

Sandra Schwabe lives with her husband in a small Indiana town. An experienced weaver, clothing designer and jewelry maker, Sandra has sold her creations at gift and dress shops in the Cleveland, Ohio and Bloomington, Indiana areas. Her household at one time included two little girls with up to two cats and a dog. Those real-life characters inspired this story.

Printed in the United States
By Bookmasters